THE GREAT GRANNY GANG

Judith Kerr

HarperCollins *Children's Books*

For my friends Virginia, Geraldine,
Diana, Heather, Tilly and Jackie

First published in hardback in Great Britain by HarperCollins Children's Books in 2012

10 9 8 7 6 5 4 3 2 1

ISBN: 978 0 00 746791 4

HarperCollins Children's Books is a division of HarperCollins Publishers Ltd.

Text and illustrations copyright © Kerr-Kneale Productions Ltd 2012

Visit our website at www.harpercollins.co.uk

Printed and bound in China

Here comes the fearless granny gang,
The youngest eighty-two.
They leap down from their granny van,
And there's nothing they can't do.

What's this? Your chimney needs rebuilding?

Old Meg will come in record time.

She is exceptionally skilled in

Repairs that may involve a climb.

Your car won't start? Maureen will fix
All faults down to the smallest rattle.

Her sister Beth, aged ninety-six,
Is known for being good with cattle.

Ballooning, Mavis Jones forgets
All else. It is her favourite sport.

Jane Pugh will baby-sit your pets.
She's not particular what sort.

And lion tamer Madge can thrill
The crowds at circuses and fairs,

While Maud, with her pneumatic drill,
Contributes much to road repairs.

One day Miss Jones, while flying low
And peering through the fading light,
Observed a robbery in full flow,
And not a single cop in sight.

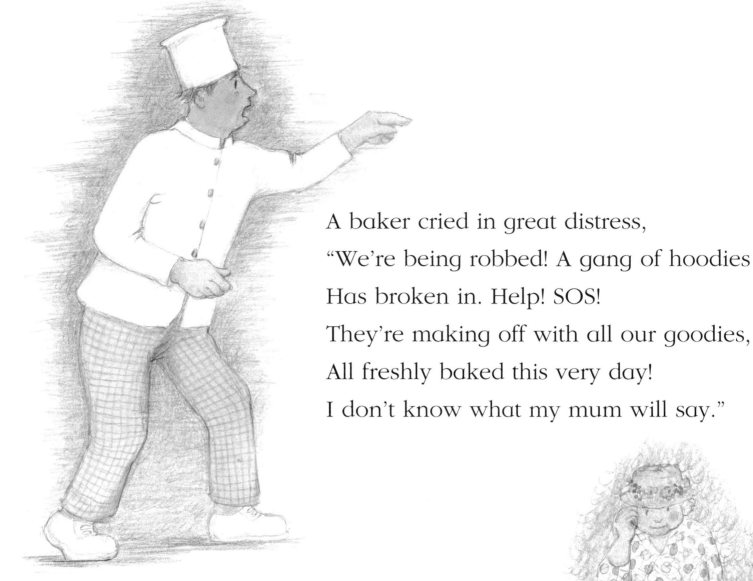

A baker cried in great distress,
"We're being robbed! A gang of hoodies
Has broken in. Help! SOS!
They're making off with all our goodies,
All freshly baked this very day!
I don't know what my mum will say."

"Granny alert!" cried Mavis Jones.
"Emergency! Prepare to raid!"
And listening on their granny phones
The grannies galloped to her aid.

Then Mavis said, "Hand back those goodies!
And fast, before my gang gets here."
Which caused the leader of the hoodies
To answer with a nasty sneer,
"Oh, little granny, how you scare me!
Oh, I'm so frightened I'm struck dumb!
Oh, little granny, please, please spare me!"

And then they saw the grannies come…

And come…

And come…

And come…

And come!

The leading hood went white with shock.

All gone the nasty sneery smile.

He stammered, "Oh! They've got a croc...

A croc... a croc... a crocodile!"

Another begged, "Oh, please, don't bite!
I will renounce my life of crime."
And then he wept, and held on tight
And hoped that lions couldn't climb.

Then all the hoods cried, "We surrender!
Your gang's the greatest, none can match it.
But we are only young and tender,
So granny, please put down your hatchet,

And please restrain that raging cow,
And do not point that dreadful drill,
For we'll be good and virtuous now,
Awash with kindness and goodwill!"

And, hoods no more, the gang took flight
And disappeared into the night.

"Well done," said Mavis. "Great success.

Congratulations to the team!"

The baker cried, "But oh! The mess!

All squidgy bits and yucky cream!

It's very sad to see my mum's

Delicious cakes reduced to crumbs."

"Nay," came a voice. "Don't worry, poppet.
I watched your little spot of bother.
I thought that batch of cakes might cop it,
And so I quickly baked another."

And there appeared
the baker's mother.

"Ladies," she said, "I've baked this banquet
To thank you. What you did was great.

So let no member of your gang quit
Until we've emptied every plate."